THOT GIRL SUMMER IN DETROIT

BY

T. FRIDAY

Dedication

This book is dedicated to the five most important people in my life, my brat pack: Jordin, Jacob, Jacory, Jakayla, and Jalisa. Please understand that everything I do and every struggle I overcome is so that you guys don't have to worry about a thing. I love you guys and don't ever forget it.

Acknowledgements

To my Blunt, you have been in my corner and stood by me for the last 15 years. Although I be getting on your nerves, you never switched up on me. Our bond is unbreakable.

To my publisher, Racquel Williams of RWP, you rock!!!! People always say make your first choice your best one, and I can say making you my first and only publisher was the best decision I could have ever made. Over the few years of working with you, I have learned so much in this industry. No matter what the situation is, you have had my back each and every way. You have shown me nothing but love, and for that, I truly appreciate you.

Jasmine Moore and Jennifer Dinwiddie, I appreciate you two for always being my listening ear when I talk about my characters as if they are real people. Y'all time is just around the corner.

To my Pen Sister Christine Davis, it's because of you that I'm doing something I love. I really appreciate you and your grind.

To my wonderful readers and my supporters, I'm nothing without you guys. For the last 4 years and 25 books later, you guys have read and reviewed all of my books, and I appreciate each and every one of you. I really just want to say thank you from the bottom of my heart. It really touches my heart when I hear some of you say I have become one of your favorite authors. You all make me keep going stronger.

To my dearest baby sister, Amanda Jordin Hollis, my white chick, I love and miss you so much. I swear 15 years wasn't long enough to have you here with us. I'd give anything to hear your voice again.

To my mom, Lisa, and dad, David, I wish you guys were here to see that I'm finally doing something I love and know for a fact that you two would be proud. I love and miss you guys so much. Please continue to watch over the family.

T. FRIDAY

CHAPTER ONE
Trina McKnight (21)

As I laid on my back with my legs resting on this fat nigga's shoulders, all I could think about was how this turned out to be my life. I couldn't lie, the money was feeding a bitch, but I was tired of using my pussy to make a living. I constantly told myself this would be the last summer I sold pussy to pay for my classes the following fall.

"Who pussy is this, bitch?" Reggie growled in my ear, like a wild animal.

Hearing that shit was irritating to my soul, but I fucked with him before and knew this fat nigga paid more when I boosted his ego. I took it as either he knew his dick was trash and needed that boost, or he really thought he was killing the pussy.

"It's yours, daddy. Yes, fuck your pussy, daddy," I moaned out with a fake, screwed up face just in case he was watching. Like I said, this nigga loved for me to play roles.

Truth be told, I couldn't feel shit, and this is why every time I fucked with him, I always went home to finish what he started. Shit, I had toys that made me wetter and fucked me better than this fat muthafucka.

"Aww, shit! I'm coming!" he moaned just after a short seven minutes of hard pumping.

Lord knows I tried so hard not to laugh in this nigga's face, but that ugly ass expression he makes when he's about to release is comical. I just couldn't hold it in any longer.

Reggie must have caught an attitude because as soon as I started laughing, he pulled his little shooter out and aimed straight towards my fucking face.

"You disrespectful, nasty ass muthafucka!" I yelled, snatching the sheet to wipe my face off.

Reggie was the one laughing now. "Is it still funny, bitch?"

I wanted to yell out, *"hell yeah, fat, little dick bitch"*, but he looked like he was ready to beat my ass. My gun was on the other side of the room, in my purse, on the dresser.

I watched as Reggie picked up my shirt to wipe off his dick. This fat muthafucka then had the nerve to toss the nasty shirt in my face like I wasn't shit. I guess, in my line of work, I wasn't.

Shit only got worse from there. Can you believe he had the nerve to walk out the door without even leaving me gas money to get home?

I got in my car feeling like I was playing the game all backwards. Instead of selling pussy, my stupid ass was handing the shit out like free candy on Halloween.

No money, no nut. I was all fucked up.

On my way home, I prayed I'd be able to leave this bullshit ass way of living for good. This couldn't be the life the Lord intended for me.

Growing up, I always wanted to own a soul food restaurant. I remember being in my grandma's kitchen, cooking with her. I've always been book smart. I guess I just picked the wrong road to travel down.

I came from nothing, but wanted everything. After high school, me and my bestie Eve attended community college, taking out student loans and shit, thinking we were gonna live our best life. But shit got hard, and with no support team behind us, we were all we had, so we had to do some shit we weren't proud of.

I was the brain out of the two and made money by doing papers for some of my classmates while Eve worked in the school library. That helped with rent and bills in our small apartment, but at the end of the day, we were starving. Truth be told, we were some ramen noodle eating muthafuckas until New Years of our freshman year.

A hot shower and some leftovers were all I needed before climbing in the bed.

It's crazy how just last night, I came home with a couple hundred, then tonight, I brought home nothing. For now, I was only gonna do business with certain muthafuckas. Not no little dick muthafucka that couldn't even make me cum. For now, it was all about me and what makes me happy.

"Turn that shit down, bitch!" I yelled, trying to bury my head in my pillow.

I loved my best friend Eve, but this bitch woke up too fucking early blasting her music. After the night I had, I wasn't in the fucking mood to hear shit, but a deposit hitting my account.

Eve popped her head in my bedroom door. "Good morning, bitch. Get dressed so we can go to breakfast."

This bitch had the perfect shape, but stayed eating.

I rolled my eyes before responding. "I'm tired and don't feel like leaving the house."

"You went out with Reggie's fat ass last night. What the fuck you tired from, faking a nut?"

Although I was still pissed about being played, I had to laugh. Eve was the sillier one out of us.

"Oh, my gawd, bitch, don't even remind me about last night. That's a whole 'nother story."

I watched as Eve walked in then flopped her ass down on my bed. "Let's talk about it at breakfast. Come on, my treat."

Hearing that this bitch was gonna pay this time, I jumped my ass up. "Give me a minute to get dressed."

That minute of getting ready turned into two hours and then picking somewhere to go. Eve and I ended up at Applebee's, eating lunch.

"So, what the fuck happened last night?" she asked, all in my business. Since this was my day one, I was ready to tell my story. Surviving a Fat Small Dick Nigga.

"Now you know how I always told you he wasn't working with shit, and I always had to fake it, right?"

"Yeah," Eve quickly replied, ready to hear my story.

"Anyways, he was making this ugly ass face and I couldn't hold my laugh in. Fat muthafucka was mad and skeeted on my fuckin' face. Then his nasty ass picked my shirt up and wiped his dick off."

Eve's face told me she was just as pissed as me, if not even more.

"Eww, bitch. I would have popped his fat ass."

"That's not even the fucked-up part," I had to warn her.

"Damn, bitch, it's more to the story?" she questioned.

I hated to tell her, but I had to. "Yes, girl, it's more. Tell me why this muthafucka walked out of the room without paying me."

"Oh, hell nah, bitch. Where was your gun? I know you ain't let him play you like that."

"My shit was in my purse on the fuckin' dresser. I'd dealt with him a few times before, so I didn't think to have it near me," I tried to explain.

I knew Eve was disappointed in me by the way she shook her head. Shit, I was disappointed too.

Let's get this straight, I wasn't 24 hours, 7 days a week hoe. I was actually paying my way through college. I thought I had a good plan to make easy money without working just as hard to get it and shit would be a straight shot to success. But I ended up hitting a few bumpy roads on the way. A bitch was tired, but I wasn't giving up.

"Now what?" Eve asked, still looking disappointed.

"To be honest, I'm sick of doing this shit anyways. If I wanna stay in school, I need to find a real job. If not, I'll be back at home with my mama, and you know I don't want that. I'm not trying to give her a reason to laugh at me."

I had so much love for Eve and every day, no matter what, she showed me why I should love her.

"You're not dropping out of school. Even if I have to double up on my dick intake, I got you."

We laughed, but she was my ride or die for real.

CHAPTER TWO

Candy (24)

Although I never sold my pussy, I hated hearing bitches talk about mismanaging theirs. I don't know why because it wasn't my business, but it irked my nerves so bad. I wanted to go sit at their table and put these little hoes on game right then and there, but there's a time and place for everything.

I was done with my salad, but I sat there a little longer sizing these girls up. They were pretty in the face with nice tits and ass for days. I knew if they fucked with me, they could make some real money. And from the sound of shit, they needed my help.

Once I saw one chick pay the bill then stand up so they could leave, I did the same. I didn't want to come off as a creep, so I tried to play it off as soon as we got to the parking lot.

"Excuse me, do one of you beautiful ladies have a lighter?"

The one named Eve shook her head no while the one that was giving out free pussy looked in her purse.

As I waited, I noticed they were label hoes from the bags to the shoes. Yeah, they had good taste, but they were rocking shit from three years ago, and it all screamed Goodwill. They needed my help to play catch up on the latest shit.

"Here you go," she finally said, handing over her red Bic.

I took the lighter then lit my blunt. "Thank you, girl. After that meal, I needed to hit this a few times. Y'all smoke?" I asked, handing over my blunt.

They stayed in the parking lot smoking with me, and just by that very action, I saw why niggas played their asses. These young hoes didn't know me from a can of paint and were cheefing my shit. What if I had laced my shit so I could kidnap they dumb asses or something?

From there, I knew how to play them.

After introducing ourselves, I pulled out my business card. "It's always nice to meet new people. I'm actually having a party this coming Saturday and wouldn't mind you two showing up. Why don't you guys call me, and I can go over the details then send you my address."

Eve was all in. "Sure, I'll be there."

Bitch was too excited, but I waited to see how Trina would respond. She seemed to be the chill one out of the two.

"What about you? I promise you're gonna have a ball," I said, trying to convince her.

It was just my luck that the dingy one of the two was on my side. "Come on, bitch, this gonna be fun. How often do we meet a cool female?"

"Alight, girl, I'm down," I heard Trina say.

Before jumping in my Range Rover and driving off, I overheard Trina tell Eve she better have fun. I smiled knowing they were gonna have fun and much more. I was about to put on my cape and save these hoes.

CHAPTER THREE
Eve Santana (21)

I searched through my closet trying to find something to wear this weekend for this party. I wasn't sure how it was gonna be, but I sure didn't wanna look like a bummy bitch in that muthafucka. I was known to be a bad bitch and needed to look such at all times.

I'd worn most of the shit I owned and needed something new. Frustrated and tired of being broke, all my clothes ended up in a pile on the floor.

Rushing in Trina's room, I started raiding her closet. "What the hell are we gonna wear tomorrow for this party?"

"I'm thinking about that short red dress that hugs my ass. Maybe I can pull a nigga or something 'cause a bitch broke."

I smiled at her decision. I felt a little jealous but smiled knowing that red dress was the shit. "Bitch, I don't have shit to wear. I wore all my sexy shit already," I whined.

Trina got up from the bed. "You the one that got a date tonight. Buy you something in the morning to wear."

I shook my head no. "I'm going out with Marcus, and you know he pays well, but I really wasn't trying to dip into my school money. Remember, we're trying to stack this summer, not spend."

Trina gave me a strange look. "Yeah, you right. Damn, what you gon' do?"

Turning my back to finish searching her closet, I let her know I would find something.

***

At 8 o'clock on the dot, Marcus was outside waiting for me to come down like clockwork.

Being married and all, this man made sure to come out to play with me at least twice a week. He kept my pockets right and stayed telling me how much he loves me. I constantly told him not to do that shit. Not only was it weird, but because of his wife. Strange thing is that shit didn't stop him at all.

Some probably question how I'm fucking a married man for money but brought up his wife when he expressed his feelings. It's simple. Business is business and feelings are never to be mixed in.

He was in love with my sexy ass and the way this little black dress fit me, I could see why. Walking out the door, Marcus was standing with the passenger side door open, waiting on me. He was a true gentleman when he wanted me to ride his face all night.

Before getting in, he tried to kiss me on the lips, knowing I don't play that shit.

"Marcus, what did I tell you about that shit?" I yelled, jumping in the car.

He got in the driver's seat. "What's the problem, baby?"

"You're married. Save those kisses for your wife."

He sat there for a minute before driving off. "I don't see why you be trippin' all the time. I love you, Eve, and ain't shit fake about that. Truth be told, I fuck you more than I fuck Tammy."

Shaking my head, I couldn't allow myself to fall for his shit. "We do business together, Marcus, that's it."

The way he started to breath heavily, I could tell he was getting pissed. "What I gotta do to have you for myself? I'll leave her and take care of you and all your problems."

I sat there thinking about the game this white dude was trying to run on me. It all sounded good, but he was married. He wasn't gonna leave that bitch for me for real, he just talked a good game. I saw this shit on TV too often.

"Let's do what we're gonna do so we can call it a night. All this shit you talkin' about makes me wanna go home."

I was lying my ass off and wouldn't dare miss out on his money, but I needed him to understand where I was coming from.

Marcus was pissed which meant he was about to pin me down to the bed and beat this pussy up. I smiled as my pussy thumped thinking about his pink dick.

That's right. I was fucking this white man and the sex is great. I was actually the first black girl he'd ever been with, and he cherished my pussy. Truthfully, if he wasn't married and could see me more than two times a week, I would only do business with him. This man paid good money and tipped even better. Sometimes I wondered what he had to offer his wife because I was getting mine.

As soon as we got into the room, Marcus pulled out a tittie and started sucking and licking all over my nipple.

"I miss you so much, Eve," he moaned out between each suck.

Him using one hand to pull my thong to the side so he could play with my clit had me dripping on his hand.

"You so fuckin' hot and wet, baby. Don't cum just yet. You gotta let daddy taste that muthafucka first."

He was so nasty, but I loved it. "Yes, daddy, come eat on this forbidden apple."

Marcus picked me up to place me in the bed, and just like that, he was eating my pussy and ass like it was his last supper.

***

I tried so hard to leave before it was too late, but after that beat down, we were walking out at check-out time.

"What are you gonna tell your wife?" It wasn't my business, but I was curious. Marcus fucked me up with his answer.

"I'ma tell her I was balls deep in the one I love."

"Stop playing with me, Marcus. I told you before that we just do business together. You keep being on that bullshit and I'm gon' cut you lose."

"I'm sorry, baby, please don't do that," I heard him beg.

Although I hated to see a grown man beg, I could tell by the look in his eyes that he was hurt by me threatening to cut him off. It was obvious this man needed my pussy to breathe.

Marcus must've been caught up in his feelings because it took him extra-long to drop me off at the apartment complex.

"Damn, we finally here. Thanks for the ride, Marcus."

"Anytime, my love."

I smiled as I watched him dig through his wallet.

"I hate that I'm married and can't have you completely to myself. I swear, just tell me when and I'll leave her for you."

With that being said, he handed over a knot of hundred-dollar bills, keep in mind he'd already given me $2000 just to spend the night with him.

"Thank you, baby."

"Baby? I knew you'd come around," he jokingly teased.

We laughed together before I got out of the car.

Going into the house, I saw Trina was still in bed knocked out. I didn't want to wake her, so I went to take a little nap myself. We had a big day ahead of us and I needed all the energy in the world for tonight.

I laid there thinking about Marcus. I constantly told myself not to fall for his shit because, in real life, a man has left his wife for a bitch who sold pussy on the side.

After a good fuck, we'd cuddle in bed and he'd remind me he was in love with me and only married Tammy because he got her pregnant and her dad sort of forced him to marry her ass. Now that the dad is dead, he felt like he didn't have to stick around any longer. I wasn't sure if he was just saying what he thought I wanted to hear, but I knew deep down inside that Marcus would take care of me and everything. Something told me I didn't want the drama that would come with him. Besides cheating with me, Marcus seemed to be a good man, and Tammy wasn't gonna let him go without a fight.

CHAPTER FOUR
Candy

"I hire you fools to do these parties twice a month. There's no way y'all should be fucking up this bad!" I yelled at the party designers.

I wasn't your average female boss, and I was the best at what I did. Jasper left my boss ass in charge for a reason.

Looking back, I wasn't a wild child growing up, but I knew what I did and didn't want. When I turned 17, I learned the true value of my pussy. Daddy wasn't in the picture and my mama didn't give a fuck about me for real. When her boyfriend at the time tried to stick his dirty dick in me while I was sleeping, I kicked his ass. I busted that muthafucka's head open with the lamp that rested on my nightstand, then ran in my mama's room looking for help. This bitch was sitting on the edge of the bed smoking a cigarette. She actually got mad because I didn't let him fuck me with his dirty dick. She cried, saying he was gonna leave her because I wouldn't act right. I had to whoop her up too before getting the fuck on. Mama or not, I didn't play that shit. If her pussy wasn't good enough for his bum ass, then he just needed to leave. I ended up on the streets for a month or so before I met Jasper.

Jasper was way older than me. I'm talking about 20 years my senior, but at the time, he was my savior. He fed me the night he picked me up from the bus bench and invited me to his home. I was scared, but it was the end of November, and it was cold as hell outside. For a week or so, I lived a good life in his baby mansion and felt like a queen. After that short period of time, I knew I never wanted to go back home or be on the streets again, and he made me feel like that would never be an option.

One night after getting out of the shower, Jasper came into my bedroom. That night, he talked to me about the type of business he was involved in. At first it scared me, but he promised nothing would happen that I didn't want to happen. After getting deeper into the conversation, I told him I was scared because I was still a virgin. He was shocked because at 17, most females had already been fucking, and some were mothers. He told me I would make even more money because I wasn't ran through, and they loved fresh meat the most. I needed the money but selling my pussy to a bunch of weird muthafuckas wasn't my thing.

Jasper thought I was stupid because I was young and had been sleeping on the streets, but I wasn't a dumb bitch. That night, I lost my virginity to him, but only after making a deal of a lifetime. He was allowed to have my virginity if I could stay there and only be his. He tossed in me helping him find other girls to work for him, and that's how I made my own money. Once his tongue touched my pussy, the deal was sealed.

Turning 18 and finally grown, Jasper asked me to marry him. He was the only man I had been with and loved, so I said yes. When I turned 22, Jasper died but was generous enough to leave everything to me, even his business. Over the years, I've been the one helping these hoes make money by throwing these parties twice a month.

My parties weren't for the broke. I had the politicians, rappers, football players, doctors and even lawyers attending, paying top dollar to fuck one of my girls. Each and every month, they sent a payment to my account just to enter my home. They paid the girls whatever they worked out and I didn't give a fuck because I got my money off top. I did have meetings to remind these girls to never lowball their pussy because these muthafuckas were paid and after a good fuck, they should be as well.

"Why aren't the bottles on ice?" I asked the bartender in disbelief.

Just as I was about to pop off, my phone rang.

"This is Candy," I softly spoke into the phone.

"Hey, this Eve. Remember you smoked some weed with me and my home girl Trina?"

I shook my head hearing Eve's ghetto ass. If I decided to keep her around, I was gonna have to work with her ass, for real.

"Oh yes, I remember," I quickly said, hoping she would get to the point.

She started ranting about them coming and trying to see what type of party it was so they could dress appropriately.

"Love, just dress your best. I must also mention that my pool and jacuzzi will be open for use tonight, so feel free to bring a swimsuit."

"Ok, this party is gonna be off the hook. We'll see you tonight."

"Alright, come prepared to have a ball." With that being said, I quickly hung up the phone.

I then went to my office to check things out. My account was extra fat, and my clientele list was popping for the night. With these two new girls, I knew things were gonna get better for me and them.

"Ma'am, I made sure each room had clean sheets on the bed and towels in the bathrooms," Sarah informed me.

"Thanks, hunny."

Sarah walked away, leaving me to my thoughts.

I often sat at this very desk where Jasper fucked me after looking at his account. I missed the fuck out of him each and every day and knew he would be so proud of me and the way I was keeping his business going strong. Sometimes I wondered if he put a curse on me. Still, to this day, he is the only man I have given my heart and pussy to. Like I mentioned before, I wasn't into selling my pussy although I was a beast at selling the next bitch's pussy. All the rich dick that swung in and out my home didn't do shit for me. Every night, I went to sleep with a rubber dick vibrating in my pussy.

Eve

"What about this one?" I asked Trina, holding up a pretty, yellow dress.

Trina gave me a strange look. This is why I hate going shopping with her. Her ass was too picky for me.

"What's wrong with it, bitch?"

"Only get that dress if you gon' walk in the party rapping, *'I got an ass so big like the sun'*."

I couldn't help but laugh. "You a petty bitch."

"I'm just saying, pick something a little safer. We don't know these people for real," she tried to explain to me.

At the end of our shopping trip, I ended up getting a little black dress. I guess black was the safest color to wear. Since I mentioned to Trina that this was also a pool party, we picked up new two-piece bikinis just in case we got in the mood.

We weren't sure how this party was going to turn out, but we still wanted to look our best. We never knew who we could run into. The way we looked at it, there was money to be made everywhere.

***

Later that night, as Trina drove to the location of the party, we couldn't help but wonder exactly where we were going. Looking at the nice houses, we knew for sure we were no longer in the hood. Even with our funds combined, we could never do it that big.

"Oh, my gawd, bitch, this is the house right there."

Looking over at the baby mansion, I was shocked. "This can't be it. Maybe that bitch gave us the wrong address and got us on a dummy mission. I know she don't stay out here."

Trina started to point. "Look at the cars pulling up over there. That has to be the party. Let's go have some fun."

After parking, we stood outside of the car, making sure we both were on point.

Trina looked good in her famous, fitted, red dress. And of course, my ass was looking plump in the black dress I found at the last minute.

"We're gonna be the baddest bitches in there tonight."

She giggled. "Ain't we always?"

"Cause periodt."

***

Stepping in, we were like kids in a fucking candy store. The layout of the house was so beautiful, and everything looked so expensive.

"She must have rented this bitch out," Trina whispered.

Before I could agree with my girl, Candy snuck up behind us.

"Actually, my late husband left it to me."

Trina was embarrassed Candy heard her and quickly tried to apologize. "I'm so sorry, girl. I just assumed that because you're our age, this couldn't have been your house."

Candy smiled. "It's ok, girl. Trust me, many don't believe me when they find out this is actually my house. By the way, I got y'all beat by a couple of years."

"Damn, bitch, you look good."

Candy smiled in between sipping on her drink.

"Thanks, Eve," she responded.

We stood there for a moment just looking around at the party guests. There were a lot of females that I had to admit were all bad, but it was the male guests that caught my attention.

"Oh my gawd, is that Big Rob, that rapper from 7 Mile?" I asked.

"Yeah, that's him. Do you wanna meet him?"

"Hell yeah, I love his music," I said, too excited.

Candy grabbed my hand then walked me across the room.

"Look, these niggas don't like all that groupie shit, so you gotta calm down. Treat this nigga like he a regular ass nigga."

"Alright, I got it," I said as I tried my hardest not to be geeked up about meeting a celebrity.

"Hey, Robert, so glad you could make it. This is my new friend Eve, and she's dying to meet you."

I stepped up so that I could say hi as she walked away.

"Hey, I'm Eve, and I love your music. Been a fan since day one," I admitted.

"How are you doing, Eve? I must admit that I have some beautiful fans."

This man was running game, and I knew not to take his words to heart. I pretended whatever he was saying to me was only for me and not a repeat from the last bitch. We took a seat at the bar to continue our conversation. He was trying to impress me by ordering the most expensive bottle they had. He was good for it, so I didn't stop him.

"How long have you known Candy? I've never seen you at one of her parties before."

"I actually just met her the other day, and she invited me and my girl to this gathering."

"So, this your first party?"

I giggled at the way he asked me that. "Yeah. Didn't I tell you I just met her like two days ago?"

Big Rob's hand left the bar top then found its way to my leg. My legs were crossed, but that didn't stop him from sliding his hand up the split in my dress. I couldn't believe my favorite rapper was trying to get fresh with me, a local nobody. Pulling me up from my seat and onto his lap, Big Rob whispered in my ear as he placed small kisses on my neck.

"Let's go somewhere quieter."

I knew what those lines meant. He was tired of the small talk and was ready to fuck. I started to wonder if Big Rob was really big like the way he rapped about in his songs. Standing up, I was ready for whatever. I allowed him to get up and lead me to one of the million rooms upstairs.

Big Rob didn't even try to get me in the bed. This nigga picked me up and sat me on the edge of the bathroom sink before quickly pulling his dick out. Having no panties on made it easy for him to reach this pussy that was dying to feel him inside of it. Moments later, he was jamming that bitch in my pussy. No foreplay, no pussy eating or nothing. This nigga was a whole fraud behind his music because his dick wasn't even that big. While his ass was rapping about 10 inches, my guess was a good 7 with a slight curve, but he was working that muthafucka.

I couldn't lie, this nigga had me folded up on the sink, beating my shit up, but my thoughts were everywhere. I couldn't help but wonder why the fuck I didn't make him wear a condom. My dumb ass wasn't that damn star struck. Or was I? As he sped up his pace, I started to push him back.

"Wait a minute!"

"Damn, shorty, what's up?" he said, slowing down just a little.

"Don't cum in me."

Big Rob started laughing. "Trust me, I won't. I'll never get caught up in all that baby mama bullshit."

Without saying shit else, he yanked me up before turning me around so he could feel this wet pussy from the back. This nigga didn't know me and I didn't know him in real life, but the way he was fucking me made me feel used and cheap. I made up my mind that once we were done, a bitch was gonna make him pay for this pussy.

"Oh shit!" he yelled out before pulling his dick out and rubbing his nut all over my ass cheek.

"Damn, I hope you didn't get that shit on my dress," I said before realizing my dress was pulled all the way up to my titties.

"Nah, shorty, you good."

As I started to stand up, Big Rob stopped me.

"Wait a minute."

He turned the water on in the tub and grabbed a washcloth from the shelf. I felt the warm washcloth wipe up his mess. At least he was thinking of me, but he still had to pay. Once I stood up to fix myself, Big Rob grabbed another washcloth so he could wash my pussy.

He then dropped both down the laundry chute.

I wasn't sure how to ask for a payment but couldn't afford not to get anything out of the deal but a wet ass.

"So, about what just happened…"

He didn't even give me a chance to respond as he pulled out a knot from his pocket. "Here you go. Maybe we can hook up at the next party."

With that being said, he walked out, not bothering to look back.

I held the money for a hot second before counting the hundred-dollar bills.

"10,000?"

Trina

Eve had left me, but I wasn't too worried because she was still at the party somewhere. Besides, after talking to Candy about taking up a business management class in school, she introduced me to this guy Gerald. He was an older guy but owned his own barber shop; two to be exact.

I knew of him from the news before. Every year, for the last three years, he had been doing those back-to-school giveaways in the hood. He would even cut the little boys' hair for free.

"So, what type of business were you looking to get into?"

I couldn't help but to smile. Besides sitting around, talking to Eve about my dreams and goals, I never had anyone ask about me.

"Although I have a few tricks up my sleeve, I wanna open a soul food restaurant."

"You must throw down in the kitchen."

"Hell yeah, I'm a beast," I said, tooting my own horn.

He smiled. "Maybe one day you can cook me dinner, and I'll be the judge of that."

"Slow down, playboy. Didn't I see you on the news with your wife and four kids?"

Gerald felt the pressure and took a sip of his drink.

"What that got to do with you makin' me a meal?"

"I never met a wife that would allow another bitch to cook for her husband."

I knew Eve fucked with married men, but I didn't.

"You lookin' too much into it, baby girl. You show me a good time with a meal included, and I'll show you how much I appreciate you with a large tip."

I sat there looking foolish. For some reason, I felt like I had the word *trick* written on my fucking forehead.

"Are you new to this type of party or something, baby girl?" he questioned.

I took a minute to look around. This shit wasn't a fucking party. It was a meet and get fucked type of party. Everything was clear now, and I understood why there were all these bad bitches talking to these older, rich-looking dudes. I was in the middle of a fucking whorehouse.

"Excuse me for a second," I said as I walked off to find Eve.

I was searching for Eve but bumped into Candy first.

"Hey, girl, can I talk to you for a second?"

"Sure, is everything ok? How are things going with Gerald?" she questioned.

I didn't say a word until we were alone in the room.

"What type of party is this?"

She played dumb. "What's the problem?"

"Is this some type of whorehouse or something? Did you invite us here to sell pussy?" I yelled in her face.

As she giggled, she pushed my hand out of her face. "Listen, little girl, I'm not forcing you or your girl to do shit y'all weren't already doing."

"What?" I asked, confused.

Now I was wondering if this bitch had been following us because she was all in our business.

"Look, y'all trying to get paid or played? Y'all both too cute to be fuckin' for pennies."

I stood there looking stupid. She did have a point.

"Look around my shit. I got all this shit and only a good, few years over than you. The real power is in the pussy. Take note and learn that shit."

With that being said, Candy walked out of the room, leaving me to my thoughts. I thought about what she said and fixed myself up before returning to the party. Once back downstairs, I saw Candy walking away from Gerald and wanted to know if they had been discussing me. With a smile on his face. Gerald walked towards me.

"I hope you have a better understanding of things now."

"Yes, everything is clear."

"So, what's the best dish you can whip up?" he asked, jumping back into the conversation we were just having.

I smile, trying to feel completely ok with what I was doing. "I love soul food, but breakfast is my favorite."

"Mine too. You know that's the most important meal of the day?"

I shook my head yeah.

Gerald grabbed me by the hand. "Let me see your moves on this dance floor."

As we danced, Gerald made sure to keep his dick pressed against my body. He wanted to fuck bad as hell.

"I can't wait to have you alone," he whispered in my ear.

I didn't say shit as I was grinding my ass on him. If it was money to be made, I was ready.

Once the song was over, I turned to face him. "I'll be right back."

He grabbed my arm to stop me. "I hope you don't get lost. I got good money for that pussy tonight."

I walked away with a fake smile on my face but really, I just wanted to talk to Eve.

"Hey, boo, you havin' fun?"

I could tell she was buzzing, which meant she was having a good time.

I pulled her out to the patio. "Do you understand what type of party this is?"

She looked at me with a straight face as if she was trying to sober up. "I didn't at first, but Candy pulled me to the side and kind of explained some things to me."

"So, how do you feel about everything?"

"Girl, just have fun and make that bread. I went off with Big Rob and that nigga threw me $10,000 just to pop this pussy over on the bathroom sink. Bitch, I ain't never made that type of money in one night. This old ass lawyer paid me $15,000 just to eat my pussy and ass. He said he had a thing for black bitches with a fat ass."

"Really, bitch? Are you serious?

"Bitch, I had to ask him how much I could get to fuck him. Shit, a bitch needed all her funds."

"What did he say?" I asked, laughing.

"He said his dick didn't get hard, that's why he could only tongue fuck me."

Now we were both laughing, and I actually felt a little better about things knowing these men had real money.

"You hooked up with anyone yet?"

"Not yet, but that guy Gerald that be all on the news wants me to leave with him tonight. What do you think?"

It didn't take Eve a second to answer. "Be careful and go make that money. I'm going straight home and will see you in the morning."

I passed over my keys to Eve so she could leave. After giving each other a hug, Candy walked her ass over to us.

"Hey, ladies. Tonight, might've been different from what you two are used to, but I'll be calling you both tomorrow to give you a better understanding of everything."

"Maybe you should've done that first," I said, still kind of pissed that she was on some sneaky shit.

"I do apologize about that. I didn't wanna scare you off when we met at the restaurant. Please forgive me and know I just wanted to help after hearing about the fat nigga running off without paying. These guys in here are paid, and if you two continue to fuck with me, you'll never have to worry about money again. Trina, I had Gerald talk to you because I knew y'all could connect with the same business mind. Play your cards right with him, and he can help you out in the long run."

Candy then looked over to Eve. "You met and fucked one of your favorite artists out. Like I said, my best interest is helping you guys out."

"I'm tired and about to head out," Eve told Candy.

"How are you getting home?"

"Since Trina got a date, I'm driving her car home." Eve replied.

"Ok, just be safe."

We watched as Eve walked off.

Candy then gave me a hug. "I promise those days of mismanaging your pussy are over."

By the time she walked away, I felt different about her and saw things her way. I turned to look for Gerald, who wasn't hard to find. He was close by, waiting on me to return.

"You ready to get out of here?"

I shook my head yeah. I didn't have any problem selling pussy. My thing was he's married. As he led me to his car, I was nervous as fuck.

"Where are we going?" I asked. I didn't want this man to take me to the house he shared with his wife and kids.

"I got a spot," he simply said.

"Oh, ok."

"I know you're new to this, and probably don't know all the rules, but families are off limits to discuss. Really, besides names, any personal shit isn't important. So, don't speak on my wife or anything else about my family," he said with a little attitude.

"Ok, I got it."

We both were quiet for a minute.

"You know, besides hearing that you were into being a business owner, I thought you were beautiful. I was happy when Candy introduced us."

I knew Gerald was trying to have a normal conversation to calm me down. He must've known I was worried and nervous. I appreciated that so much.

Finally getting to the condo where I assumed he took all his side bitches, I was ready to make my money. Walking in the door and looking around, "bachelor pad" screamed through my head.

"Nice crib."

"Thanks," he said, pulling me in for a hug.

This dude had to be in love with my ass 'cause no matter what was going on that night, his hands always found a way to squeeze an ass cheek.

"You can follow me, so we can get a little more comfortable."

I started to follow him into the bedroom before he stopped.

"Damn, girl, you got my mind gone. My ass almost forgot something."

"What's that?" I questioned.

Gerald held his hand out. "You gotta hand over the cell phone."

"What?"

"Yeah, it's to protect me and my family."

I shook my head in agreement before pulling my phone out of my purse. I wasn't the type to fuck and run my mouth, but I understood he had a lot to lose if it got out that he wasn't shit.

Entering the room, Gerald picked up his remote and music instantly started to play. He was some type of old school playboy, and you could tell. Gerald slowly pulled my dress down to the floor so I could step out of it.

"Spin around for me, baby girl. Let daddy see all that ass," he ordered.

Like a good girl, I did what he asked. I turned around a few times just to tease Gerald. Finishing my final twirl, Gerald grabbed me by the waist before pulling me closer to him. I usually didn't allow kissing on my dates, but the man had his tongue so far down my throat, I could barely breathe.

"You alright?" he asked once I finally broke free from him.

"Yeah, I'm good."

Gerald walked me over to the bed. He took a seat but wanted me to stand up.

"You gotta work for this money. Strip for me, baby."

Slowly dancing in his face, I grind my ass in his face, causing his dick to poke out of his drawers. Next, my bra was being tossed across the room.

"Damn, baby girl, you got me ready to empty my account for that ass."

I learned when I first started this lifestyle that muthafuckas would say anything for the pussy, so his words didn't mean shit to me. I was gonna do what I had to for my bread then dip on his ass.

That night, I learned Gerald was an old ass freak. That man sucked and fucked on every inch of my body. Just looking at him, you'd never guess he had it in him.

***

Feeling the sun burn down on my naked body, I jumped up.

"Damn, I gotta go," I mumbled.

Gerald must have felt me get up because his ass jumped up too. "Where do you think you're going?"

"Home," I simply answered.

Gerald chuckled. "Nah, baby girl, you owe me breakfast."

That man spent all night and half of the early hours pinning me down on the bed, fucking the shit out of me. I don't know how he thought I had the energy to cook breakfast too. I wasn't a fucking robot.

"Are you serious?"

"Hell yeah, I'm serious. After tearing that wet pussy up, I need food to build up my energy. I got an interview in a few hours."

After a shower, Gerald gave me a t-Shirt to put on so I could cook his breakfast. Tired and all, I took my ass in that kitchen and slaved over the hot stove. I needed money for school and couldn't be picky on how I was gonna make it.

I got in my Uber leaving Gerald's stomach full of cheesy eggs, grits with shrimp and fish. He enjoyed his meal which got me a bonus. Arriving home, I counted out $35,000. I know I didn't wanna do this shit at first, but the money was just right, and a bitch couldn't complain.

CHAPTER FIVE
Candy

Maybe I was wrong for the way I just tossed Eve and Trina into the jungle, but I bet those hoes made more money than they ever did on their own. The night of the party, Eve is the one who jumped right into it. She had no idea what type of party this was, but she didn't care to find out. Eve wanted to get fucked, and she got just that; any payment was extra.

Truth be told, I liked her because she was true to herself. Now Trina, on the other hand, was different. She tried to act like she was mad about the type of party I invited her to, but she left with a muthafucka. Most girls that were nervous or whatever would have made their money in one of the rooms upstairs and called it a night. Bitch acted like she was too good for my party but went off to get dicked down. I bet her ass was gonna be at the next party as well.

Today I was gonna call the girls and invite them to dinner or something so I could see where their heads were after their first night of doing one of my parties. The guys were digging the newbies, and I knew there was money to be made. Seeing that it was now 2:30pm, I decided to give them a call. I was pretty sure they'd slept off the night before and were ready for a new day. After the fourth ring,

Eve answered her phone. I made the decision to call her first because she seemed to a little bit more down to earth.

"Hello."

"Hey, Eve, this is Candy. I wanted to invite you and Trina to dinner at my place tonight. There's no secret agenda behind this, and it will only be the three of us outside of my staff."

I could tell over the phone that Eve was all smiles. Little bitch was down for whatever.

"That sounds like a great idea. I'll talk to Trina about it and see what she thinks. I'll call you back a little later."

"That sounds like a plan."

Once we got off the phone, I went into my office to check on my bank account. Last night's party was a success and from the early deposits that were hitting my account for the next party, I knew it was gonna be even better.

Knowing these girls weren't about to turn down a free meal, I let my cook know we were having extra guests for dinner that night.

After logging out of my account, I made my way downstairs to get my daily massage. This was one of the best moments of my day besides watching my account grow.

Maria had been around since Jasper was alive, and I understood why he kept this bitch around. Every day, after a long, hot shower, I would put on my robe just to take it off and have her massage my body. I know I mentioned before that I hadn't been with a man since Jasper died and used toys, but Maria was the best head doctor ever. That bitch could suck all my stress away out of my asshole.

I didn't have to say shit to her. I simply dropped my robe and climbed on the massage table. Maria liked to rub me down with this hot oil that felt so good sinking into my skin. While massaging the oil on my juicy booty, she always managed to slip a finger or two inside my pussy. I can't lie, that shit turned me completely on. Enjoying her hands on my body, I thought back to the first time she turned me out. I was 17, and she had to be about 29 at the time.

I had been staying with Jasper for a good two months when he introduced me to his personal massage therapist, Maria. Later that night, Jasper went out claiming he had some business to handle, but whatever. It probably had something to do with another bitch, but that's a whole other story. Maria met me in the kitchen and suggested I let her give me a massage since I looked stressed out. I had no idea what she had in store for me that night.

"Just lay flat on your back, and I'll make you feel better," she ordered.

After removing my clothes, I did as told. Being broke and from the hood, I never had the pleasure of getting a real massage. Truth be told, I never had anyone touch me the way I allowed Jasper to touch me. Everything was going good until I felt Maria's oily fingers slide in my pussy.

"What the fuck!" I yelled, causing her to panic.

"I apologize, ma'am. Please don't tell Mr. Jasper on me. I just couldn't help myself. You're just so beautiful."

I wanted to slap that bitch 'cause I wasn't into bitches, especially older, Mexican bitches. Still, she kept playing with my pussy as she apologized, making me wetter than I'd ever been before.

Once she flipped me over on the table, Maria buried her face in my pussy, making me moan out. If anyone heard me, they would've thought I was downstairs taking 10-inch pipe.

She eased up a little then whispered, "Don't run, ma'am, I'll make you so happy just like I do for Mr. Jasper."

Did this bitch really just admit to fucking around with Jasper? Yeah, she did, but I couldn't get mad. I opened my legs wider, so she could dive right back in. I wanted to feel as good as Mr. Jasper's cheating ass.

I laid there letting this lady have her way with me and never told a soul. It was our little secret, or so I thought. The next morning, Jasper was up in his office. I thought he was going over some work, but to my surprise, he was watching Maria suck on me.

"Candy! Candy, get your ass up!" he yelled, standing in the doorway.

I jumped up, not knowing what he was pissed off about. I followed him as he stormed out of the bedroom and into his office.

"This the type of shit you doin' in my house?" he questioned as the video played out on the computer.

I'd never been in this type of situation and didn't know what to say, so I stood there like a fucking mute.

Jasper was pissed and jumped up, slapping the shit out of me. "Bitch, do you hear me talking to you?"

"Sorry, I didn't know that was gonna happen. I just wanted a massage." I let those words come out as soon as the video showed me on all fours, spreading my ass cheeks open for Maria to fuck my ass with her tongue.

Jasper laughed at me. "I don't own you, but if that's what tip you on, let me know something. In this house, I have two rules for you to follow. One, never give my pussy away to another nigga, and two, never lie to me."

I was still quiet and embarrassed.

"So, was it good?"

I was scared to tell him it was the best head I'd received knowing he and Maria were the only ones to ever do that to me, so I lied. "No, I didn't like it."

Jasper chuckled before slapping me again. "You're still lying in my face."

I watched as he stepped out the room. I could overhear him telling someone to send Maria up to his office. I was so scared and just knew he was about to beat both our asses before putting us out on the street. Lord knows I wasn't ready to go back home. Maria walked in with Jasper right behind her. She was scared and never looked me in the eyes.

"Maria, Candy said she didn't enjoy the massage last night."

I couldn't believe how he put me on spot like that.

"I'm sorry, I tried my best, I really did."

Jasper walked over to me, making me to flinch, thinking he was about to fuck me up for real. Instead, he lifted my head to give me a kiss.

"Take your clothes off," he whispered in my ear.

I was scared but listened. As I undressed, he stood there next to Maria, watching my every move. I saw him whisper to Maria, and she started to undress as well.

"Maria, go ahead and show me how you did her last night. Candy, I want you to tell me what you didn't like."

"Jasper, this is crazy."

"Shut your ass up before I take you back to the bus stop!" he yelled.

Scared of going back to being homeless, I laid on the couch in his office and cocked my legs open for Maria. Just like last night, she drove me crazy and had me moaning out. Jasper sat in his seat watching with his dick in his hand. This nigga was turned on and couldn't control himself.

"Alright, Maria," he called out as my legs began to shake. "Candy, did you enjoy that?"

This time, I decided to tell the truth. The way my legs were still shaking after the fact, there's no way to say I didn't. "Yes, I did."

"Good. Maria, for now, your job is to make sure me and Candy are completely satisfied."

Even though he saw me on tape enjoying Maria's work, he still made her do that shit in front of him. Jasper could be such an asshole sometimes. I thought I was gonna be able to leave, but he made me sit in his chair to watch Maria suck his dick until he nutted down her throat. I now understood why he got massages every day and never asked me for head.

Now, years later, she has always been my go-to person. She would massage me until I dozed off then eat me until I woke up. Whenever I needed a little extra attention, she was there to save the day. Maybe I'll let her give Eve and Trina a massage as an appreciation for all the hard work she put in over the years.

Eve

"So, how was your night?" I asked, taking a seat on Trina's bed.

"Bitch, I made just about enough to pay for my first semester with that guy Gerald. At this point, fuck all my old clients."

I was surprised to hear Trina say that shit, but she was right. One night put the amount of money in our pockets that we were probably making in months.

"I think I'll keep Marcus around, but fuck everyone else," I had to admit.

We both giggled.

"Bitch, if we keep doing this, we can finally move into a better place and get a new car," Trina pointed out.

I agreed to that. We were kind of sharing the car she had, and it worked out a little, but having my own shit would be cool.

"So, Candy called me earlier."

"What the fuck did she want?" Trina asked.

"She wants us to come over for dinner. She said she wanted to talk to us about last night. Do you wanna go?"

"I do wanna go. I know I was mad at first, but she was right about some stuff. Last night, we did what we were used to doing, but only for muthafuckas with real money."

I was happy she was seeing things my way. "Girl, that's what I'm saying. We were just fuckin' a nigga for a hot $200. Dealing with her, I made bread letting an old muthafucka lick this pussy. Ain't no way in the world I'm going back to the old days."

"So, is this what we gon' do?"

"Hell yeah, bitch!"

Trina gave me a serious look. "If you down, I'm rolling too."

After taking a shower and getting dressed, Trina and I decided to go shopping. We wanted to look cute for dinner with Candy. She claimed there wasn't a hidden agenda, but there's no telling with her ass. That day, we were finally about to walk in the store and pay for whatever we set our eyes on without looking at a price tag. If this is how our life was gonna be from now on, I had no problem dealing with Candy.

***

"Bitch, you look good in that dress. I swear red is definitely your color."

I turned to face Trina. "Thanks, boo. You look good too."

We stood in my full-size mirror examining ourselves. We were both two bad bitches, but now with money.

"You ready to go see what our boss wants?"

"Hell yeah, but I got a feeling she just wanna make sure we're still on good terms after her little party."

"The way I look at it, that bitch just put us on," Trina added.

"You right, bitch, but let's be on our way. You know this bitch live far as fuck."

I now understood how she could afford this big ass house and shit. That bitch only had a few years over me and Trina, but I wanted to be like her. We stepped in then heard someone call out to Candy that her guests had arrived. An older white guy then came out.

"Please follow me."

We did as told and followed him into the dining room. Candy was seated at the head of the table and me and Trina took a seat on both sides of her.

"Welcome, ladies. I'm so happy you could make it. No hard feelings, I hope?"

I was the first to speak up. "Hell nah, girl, you really looked out for us."

Trina took her turn to speak up. "Although you could've been straight up with us, I did end up making more money than I've ever made in one night, so I can't be mad about that."

"To be honest, when I overheard you two talking over lunch about niggas running off with pussy and how broke you two were, it was only right to help out. I hate to see women in this game being over sexed and under paid. I do apologize for misleading you two, but I wasn't sure how to be upfront with you."

I understood where she was coming from 'cause I wouldn't have known how to ask someone if they wanted to attend a party to sell pussy either.

We sat around eating fat, juicy steaks and drinking some of the best champagne there was. I felt like if Trina was down and saw no flaw in this shit, then I was down for the ride right by her side.

Trina

After dinner, a bitch was buzzing and full. I was ready to take a nap. While I chilled in the recliner, I watched Candy and Eve dance around, just enjoying the night.

"Come on, Trina, come play with us!" Candy called out.

"I'm good. Besides, I'm really not a big drinker, and I'm fucked up right now."

Candy walked over to me. "I know what you need," she said with a grin.

If that bitch knew what I really needed, she'd pull a nigga with a big dick out of her pocket, but instead, she left then returned to the room with this Mexican chick.

"Trina, this is Maria. She is my personal massage therapist and trust me, she will get you together."

Maria reached out her hand to help me out of the chair. To be honest, I could go for a good massage. A bitch never had a real one before.

"Come with me, ma'am, I'll make you happy."

I turned around to look at Eve, but that bitch was dancing and drinking out the bottle. I knew I was driving home that night.

"Go ahead and undress, I'll give you a second," Maria ordered.

Getting undressed was easy since I was only wearing a dress. It was too fucking hot for anything else. Just as promised, Maria returned to work her magic.

"This oil is a little warm but will relax your whole body," she warned.

"Okay, I'm cool with that."

Maria got to work on my legs and feet, and that shit alone had me dozing off. What made me try to get up is when my toes felt wet. I know this bitch wasn't sucking on my toes.

"What the hell?" I yelled out, trying to sit up.

"No, no, no, ma'am. Lay back down, I'll make you happy," she said again.

Not sure if that happened was for real or if it was me dozing off had left me a little clouded, I laid back down.

I wasn't sure how long I had been asleep, but I woke up hearing myself moan out. "Mmmm."

"Yes, I can make you happy," I heard her whisper.

"What the fuck are you doing?"

Maria continued to suck on my clit as if I wasn't even talking to her. As I tried to get up, I could feel her hand holding my lower back down on the table.

"Maria, stop," I finally called out.

Maria was really enjoying herself. She had one finger in my pussy while sucking my soul away.

"I'm sorry. You're just so beautiful, and I couldn't help myself."

I sat there confused. Never in life had I been attracted to a female. I still wasn't but damn, she knew what the fuck she was doing, and I liked it. Instead of going off or getting up to leave, I laid my ass back down on the table, but this time, I flipped over on my back.

Maria opened me back up and didn't hesitate to finish her job.

CHAPTER SIX

Candy

Now that Trina was out of the picture, I could play with Eve. During dinner, Trina seemed to be cool with everything, but I still wanted Eve's sexy ass to myself.

"Damn, girl, do I need to go get another bottle or what?" I asked, knowing damn well she didn't need shit else to drink.

"Oh my gawd, bitch, no," she said, stumbling to the couch.

I took a seat next to her. "You are very beautiful."

Her words slurred, "Thanks, you are too."

I still had my glass in my hand, taking sips, watching her slowly doze off. "Aht, aht, bitch! You're not about to go to sleep on me. Get up and play with me."

She sat up a little, giggling. "I'm buzzing like a muthafucka right now, Candy."

I wasn't trying to hear that shit. I've wanted her since day one, and I always got what I wanted. Sliding my hand under her dress, I smiled seeing the bitch didn't have on any panties.

"Oh, so that's what tip you on tonight?" she said with a grin on her face.

"That's only if you're down for a good night."

I stood up from the couch and helped her drunk ass get up. I never fucked none of these bitches in my room, but with twelve other rooms in the house, space was never a problem.

Picking Eve out of the two was the best decision I ever made. She was a real-life freak and not scared to be herself. Not only was she open to fucking around with me, she didn't mind me using my strap on her. This bitch took it in every hole and that's something most hoes were against. I couldn't wait to add that to her profile. These niggas were gonna have to double up on my money for this one.

"Oh shit," I heard her moan out.

I had her bent over on all fours with my strap in her ass while having her hold a vibrator in her pussy. I giggled as this bitch squirted all over the bed. She was going crazy like a raging bull.

"Next time, I gotta try that on you," she said as we climbed out of the shower.

I was blushing. "So, it's gonna be a next time?"

"That's all up to you, Candy. I mean, you the one that started this shit," she responded.

"I would like to see you before our next party later this month. If you have to bring your friend, I'll have a way to keep her out of our way."

When we finally made it back downstairs, Trina was just coming back from her massage.

"Damn, girl, you look so stress free. That massage must've been magical," Eve teased.

Trina had a small grin on her face. "Yeah, it was. Are you ready to go because it's late as hell?"

"Yeah, I'm ready if you are," Eve responded.

I walked them to the door.

"It was nice of you to invite us to dinner, we appreciate it."

I gave them both a hug. "I'll be reaching out to you both about the next party and I hope to see you both there."

"For sure, girl."

Eve

The car ride seemed awkward. We usually talked about everything, but that drive home was too quiet. I wasn't sure how to tell her what happened between me and Candy.

"What's on your mind?"

"Life," she simply said, very dry.

"You know you my bitch, you can talk to me," I assured her.

"Eve, tonight, I allowed some shit to happen that I really don't think I wanna do again. I'm not happy with myself right now."

She was getting on my nerves playing around instead of just coming out and saying what she gotta say. "What's wrong, bitch? What the fuck happened?"

"When I went downstairs for the massage, that Maria bitch ate my pussy."

I tried not to laugh, but the way she said it tickled me. "What?"

"Bitch, I'm serious. That bitch was rubbing me and when I woke up, she had her face buried in my pussy, going to work."

"I'm confused. Are you complaining or did you enjoy the shit?"

Trina started to laugh. "Bitch, I don't know. You know I don't fuck with bitches, but I can't lie, that shit felt good. She just kept saying, *'I'll make you feel good, ma'am'.*"

I kept laughing. "So, did she?"

"Hell yeah, and I came all over that bitch's face," Trina said, laughing.

"Was she mad at you?

"Hell nah! That bitch kept sucking on me like a fucking pacifier."

"Bitch, are you serious?" I asked, laughing.

She stopped laughing for a second. "Soon as I realized what happened, I jumped up from the table. Bitch caught me slippin'."

For the rest of the ride, we talked about how Maria got down, but I couldn't tell her what happened between me and Candy. For some reason, I thought she would judge me or something. I usually didn't care 'cause we thotted together many times, but this time felt different.

Trina had been my bitch since day one. We were always about getting our money together. I remember when we went out with these two brothers. These niggas didn't even care enough to get separate rooms. Me and my bitch were getting fucked on the same bed by these brothers and didn't give a fuck when they switched up on us. We took both dicks and enjoyed our night. We did a lot of thotting together, but still, something was different about this night.

***

The next afternoon, after a hot shower, I laid across the bed thinking about Marcus' ass, but only because he'd been blowing my phone up like crazy. This might sound strange, but I was all fucked out and not in the mood to fuck with him that night. Now you know something had to be up if my ass wasn't in the mood to fuck

"Damn, dude, give me a fucking break," I bitched as I finally answered the phone after seeing he wasn't gonna stop calling.

"Hello," I said, giving much attitude.

"Good afternoon, my beautiful queen. I can't wait to see you later."

I rolled my eyes. He knew how to kiss ass for sure.

"Good afternoon, Marcus. How can I help you?"

"Marry me, my love."

I started to laugh, this man didn't give up knowing he was married, and we were only business associates.

"Marcus, stop playing with me before I tell Tammy on your ass."

"Go ahead, I'm begging you. Maybe then she will leave me for good. I went home the other morning smelling just like your sweet pussy, and she didn't say shit. I didn't shower until that night and nothing happened."

"Marcus, you're crazy. I swear you have a problem."

"I'm only for you and your love. I have a surprise for you tonight."

I hated to burst his bubble, but I wasn't in the mood to hook up with him. "Marcus, about tonight, I'm so tired. I think I'm gonna have to reschedule."

"Nah, that can't happen. I'll pay you double just to chill with me tonight. To sweeten the deal, you won't even have to fuck me, just let me taste my forbidden apple."

How could I turn down double pay just to get sucked on? I wasn't that type of dummy.

"What time are you coming to pick me up?"

"How does 7pm sound?"

"Alright, just call when you're outside."

Since I didn't have shit else to do, I decided to nap until it was time for me to get ready.

Just as I was dozing off, Trina came into my room.

"Move over, bitch."

"Girl, you see me trying to rest, go get in your bed," I said playfully, pushing her away.

Trina's irritating ass held on to me. "But I love you, bestie. I'm not going nowhere."

We both laughed.

"What do you want, girl?" I asked.

"The school is starting to drop classes on their site. Let's get ahead of these muthafuckas and find our classes now."

"Girl, I'm not in the mood for that school shit right now."

"Okay, I'm about to handle my business, but don't be mad when all the good classes are gone."

After she left, I closed my eyes. Truth be told, if this party shit worked out over the summer, my ass wasn't gonna stay in school. Candy was living the dream and that bitch wasn't giving a school her hard-working money, so why should I? That's another thing I didn't wanna talk to Trina about. It seemed like we were going in two different directions now.

***

Like clockwork, Marcus was in front of the building, waiting for my sexy ass to come down.

"Damn, you look so good, I just wanna bite your ass," he said, rubbing my ass as I got in the car.

"So, what's my surprise?" I asked as he drove off.

"I'll tell you when we get downtown to the room."

Marcus never took me anywhere cheap. He would never pay for one of those $75 rooms. When it came to me, he didn't mind spending whatever. I played it off, but I couldn't wait to see my surprise. Marcus could be so romantic and that's one of the reasons I kept coming back to him besides the money. I never had a real boyfriend that did romantic shit with me. These niggas only liked to fuck on me and cheat.

The room was filled with rose petals and candles. I couldn't help but to blush.

"You're so sweet, Marcus."

"Anything for you, my love."

Marcus had a problem remembering he was married with all that love shit.

"What's my surprise, Marcus?"

"Calm down, baby, it's coming," he said, undressing.

I know for sure he remembered me saying I didn't feel like fucking tonight. My face must have said a lot because Marcus caught on really quick.

"No worries, I know you're tired and don't wanna fuck but as promised, I just wanna please you tonight."

After taking my dress off, Marcus ordered me to lay on my back so he could make me happy. This man licked and sucked on every inch of my body. That night, he was my personal washcloth.

"Damn, Marcus, you got me about to cum again."

Saying that only made him suck on me even harder. This man really wanted to eat me alive and if there was a way, my ass would've been gone.

"Marcus," I moaned out as I came again.

"I love you so much, Eve."

I didn't care how good he made me feel, I wouldn't allow those words to come out my mouth. I loved Marcus' money, dick and head, but I couldn't love a married man. In my feelings, I finally pushed his head away from me.

"What's wrong, baby?"

"Marcus, you gotta stop telling me that shit."

"I can't help the way I feel about you, Eve. I love you and want you to be mine."

I couldn't deal with the shit any longer. I climbed out the bed to put my dress on. I found a way to get money and didn't have to deal with Marcus' ass any longer. I was trying to be nice and keep him around, but he was getting on my nerves, trying to pressure me into being his girl.

"What are you doing, Eve?"

"I played this game long enough with you, Marcus. Yes, I was wrong, but I can't keep sleeping with you. Go home to your wife tonight."

"Wait, Eve! What about your surprise?"

My greedy ass turned around to face him. "What is it, Marcus?"

I watched as he walked over to his pants on the chair. He then pulled out a ring box while dropping down on one knee.

"Marry me, Eve. I promise I'll take good care of you."

"Marcus, get up. I don't know why you don't understand that I can't marry you while you're still married. Just go home to your wife and let's say this was a freebie. I gotta go."

Marcus sat on the bed crying while I got myself together. I hated to leave him like that, but he was doing the most.

"Eve, please, just give me one more chance," he begged.

"I'll catch an Uber home. You need to go home to your family and forget about me."

As I shut the door, I could hear him screaming like a mad man and throwing things. I hurried to the elevator to set up my ride. I needed to get away from him by any means.

In the lobby, while waiting on my ride, I prayed Marcus didn't come down there and make a scene. I'd hate for him to embarrass the both of us. Once the Uber, on my way home, I deleted his number from my phone. At this point, I had no choice but to cut him completely out of my life. The money was always good, but he broke the number one rule of mine and that was falling in love with me. I was a thot that sold pussy. I wasn't brought into this world for love.

CHAPTER SEVEN

Candy

I had a longtime friend that came into town with his buddy at least four times a year, and they needed some excitement in their life. I know from the videos that I secretly recorded and watched that these men were lovers and loved dicks with a dash of pussy on the side. They paid top dollar for the nastiest, freakiest, hoe I had. Since I had already tested Eve out, I decided to call her up instead of using her to entertain me. I told them I had a girl on deck that was down for whatever as long as they had their bread stacked, and of course, I needed my finder's fee upfront. Everything was good on their end, now I just had to pull her in. She answered the phone on the third ring.

"Good afternoon, sexy."

I could tell I had woken her up, and she was blushing. All my girls were happy when they thought they were my favorite.

"Hey, Candy! What's up, boo?"

"Listen, I have a job set up with an old friend of mine and thought that it would be perfect for you."

Eve hesitated to respond as she gave it a little thought.

"If you're not ready to be a big girl and make this money, just say that shit. I can always call one of these other bitches that's been in the game a little longer, but they'll pay more for a fresh face," I said just to see if I could get her to break.

"What time and where?"

I smiled knowing my plan worked. "Just come to my house in the next hour or so, and I'll help you get prepared for them."

"Them?" she questioned.

I didn't have time for her bullshit and trying to pull out now. "I'll see you in a few."

I hung up before giving her all the facts. I always allowed my closest friends to use one of the many rooms in my home. I got a kick out of going back and watching their fuck sessions when I was bored.

Laughing to myself, I realized Jasper had turned me into some type of pervert. I had to admit that something was seriously wrong with me. It had to be because I'd rather watch people get fucked than let another man touch my body in any type of way. Thank God for Maria.

***

Eve came to my door in exactly an hour looking nervous as fuck.

"Hey, I just wanted to say thank you for calling me. I need this extra money, but what's this shit about? You said *them*, not *him*."

I walked back to the couch. "Follow me, sweetie."

After we took our seats on the couch, I ordered Jessica to bring us a bottle of champagne.

"Tonight, one of my old buddies will be in town with a close friend of his. These guys are major freaks and only like to be hooked up with freak bitches that can handle multiple dicks at one time. Are you the right girl for this job?" I questioned.

"I'm not no armature to taking dicks, Candy. I can handle them."

She looked scared, but I wasn't about to let her ass back down now.

"Don't disappoint me, Eve. These guys spend good money every time they come to Detroit for business. If you do good at pleasing them, they'll always ask for you and keep your pockets right."

I could tell that she was still a little nervous and might have bitten off more than she could chew, but she was a bitch that was about making her money. Yeah, I could have dismissed her and found one of my regulars, but since she wanted to play this game, I was about to deal her in.

Eve

Candy had me shook. I have let two niggas run a train on me before, a few times, but she was talking like these niggas had dicks the size of a tree trunk or something. That afternoon, I made sure to show up to her house a little early so we could talk about my date for the night. As she talked about her buddy and his friend, I sipped on my drink. Being drunk always brought out my alter ego and made the scared, young girl disappear. After another shot, Candy walked me upstairs to one of the bedrooms.

"For your protection and privacy, I've allowed you all to use this room for your date."

I looked around at how nice the room was set up.

"It's nice in here. I can't wait to get my money together so I can get a nice house like this."

I noticed the strange look on Candy's face but didn't say shit. "The connected bathroom is right over here."

I peeked in the bathroom and instantly fell in love. This bathroom was so much better than the one Big Rob fucked me in. Stepping back in the room, I watched as Candy pulled out a shopping bag.

"These items are for you. Please use everything in here tonight."

She left the room so I could have some privacy. I shook my head looking at the bullshit in the bag. Inside contained some handcuffs, a dildo, a butt plug and some anal ease.

"Hell nah, what the fuck?"

Now I was thinking about backing out and taking my black ass home. I paced the floor, debating if I really wanted to go through with this shit. Her buddy was gonna have to find another bitch to bust open. I'd had my fair share of dicks, but from the shit in that bag, these muthafuckas were on some other shit.

Candy walked back into the room. "Hey, don't be nervous, boo. I know you're the best bitch for this job."

I shook my head in agreement.

"This right here is your new best friend. Take this bitch, and the rest of the day will go smooth."

She stood there waiting for me to take the pill with the rest of my wine. I usually wasn't into taking pills, but with her watching me like a hulk, I tossed it in my mouth and swallowed it down with my drink.

"Good girl. Now after you freshen up, just relax, and they'll be here in no time. Show my friend how Detroit bitches get down."

Relaxing in the tub, I started to feel how Ebony felt at Junior's bachelor party. In the pit of my stomach, something told me it was gonna be a crazy night. Feeling faded and ready to lay down, I finally got out of the tub. I swear I didn't feel like doing shit but going to sleep. I guess the pill was starting to work. I laid across the bed praying I got a nap in before these muthafuckas got here.

***

Soon as I felt my body slip into a good sleep, I was awakened by two black guys tapping me. I knew it was time to get to work by the way they were both butt ass naked, stroking their dicks. These muthafuckas ain't come to play. I checked out what they were working with before looking over at Candy who was standing there with a smirk on her face.

"James and Thomas, this is one of the new beautiful girls I was telling you two about."

"Yeah, she is beautiful, but I'm trying to see what that mouth do," James said, rubbing his dick across my lips.

I felt so disrespected but smiled like everything was ok. Even the hood niggas I dealt with in the pass never just slapped my lips with their dick before.

Candy must've seen I didn't like that and tried to make sure I didn't fuck up what she had going on.

"Ok, y'all, play nice."

"For sure, love. You know we're good guys," Thomas assured.

Candy leaned over, placing a kiss on my lips.

"They're gonna take good care of you as long as you playfair.

After that, Candy walked out the room, leaving me with these guys who acted like they hadn't had pussy in years. I knew they were about to fuck the shit out of me, with they thirsty asses.

"What you waitin' for, girl? Wet them lips up and suck this dick," James ordered.

Trying to act like I wasn't uncomfortable, I did as I was told. I slowly took it in inch by inch. This man was packing, but I was about to show this nigga they weren't about to "little girl" me. I was a whole, grown ass woman.

"That's right, bitch. Suck that dick, you nasty hoe."

James talked too much shit for me but turned into a little bitch when I was sucking him up and Thomas started eating his ass. Never in my life had I fucked with two nigga that fucked on each other too. At first, I was disgusted, but after a while, that shit was lit. Having two guys cater to your body just as much as they catered to each other was something new for my ass. But once it was all said and done, I walked out the house the next morning feeling refreshed and with a fat pocket. I couldn't wait until they came back to town in a few months.

CHAPTER EIGHT

Candy

I was somewhat crushing on Eve when I first met her but now, I felt sorry for her. I had all intentions on helping her make money. I really did, but she was too eager to do whatever for money, and the shit was low key sad.

I watched Thomas and James double dick this thot down, then dick each other down. She didn't have a care in the world as long as she knew she was gonna make money. Not only was she quick to jump on this opportunity too fast, but she never even asked how much she was gonna get paid to be these muthafuckas' sex slave overnight. James handed over a total of $150,000, and Eve walked away with only $50,000.

The next morning, after watching their sex tape and coming multiple times, I took a long shower then got dressed. My goal was to go out and find some new girls for the next party. I had a good feeling Trina was gonna stay strictly business while Eve was gonna crash and burn pretty soon. I hate to speak so negatively about a bitch that I once put my lips on, but she was the type of thot bitch to do a line if a nigga had the right amount of money in her face. In my line of business, I'd seen it all and knew niggas would turn a bitch out on that dick and nose candy just to have something to brag about.

My first stop was this ghetto ass mall. From what I learned, bitches loved the mall. They all loved walking around, looking and dressing the same. This shit always reminded me of when Jasper had my ass in these malls picking up bitches that were looking to make some money.

The first few times I did it, I was scared shitless. I just knew a bitch was gonna think I was weird or something. I called myself being a boss bitch, stepping to this one chick in the shoe store. She was really tall and slim, but very pretty. She went the fuck off on me so bad. I still remember running out the store, scared to get my ass beat.

I went home with no new pussy to offer, and Jasper tore my ass up. His favorite shit to yell at me when he beat my ass was that he would send me back to the streets or sell my pussy to the highest bidder. After fucking up two more times and getting my ass beat, I was tired and knew I had to find a way to pull in the perfect, vulnerable female to do some work. After practicing for a week straight, I went out one day and had three bitches ready to come to the party. I actually think one of them still works for me after all this time.

One day, I must've had a higher power on my side. This pretty, chocolate bitch fell straight in my lap, basically begging for help. Long story short, I found her in the restroom crying, so I played the concerned, big sister role. She cried about losing her job and when she told her boyfriend, he basically broke up with her, and kicked her out the house, saying he only dated chicks with money. I felt bad for her and wanted to take her to that nigga's house to beat his ass myself.

After getting her to calm down, I played Jasper's role. I treated Tamia to a meal then took her home that night. She stayed there with me and Jasper for a whole week before he was in her room, breaking down the rules to her. She didn't act too scared or nervous to pop that pussy for some money. To my surprise, she was working two days later at the party. Tamia worked for us for three months before she was able to get her own place and move out. She worked for us for a whole two years before she was killed by a local ball player. He had paid for Tamia each and every party and one day, his wife found out about him banging her young ass. His wife threatened to divorce him and take everything. He was so fucked up that he ended up killing Tamia.

Let me just say this, and this will be my first and last time talking about it. I found out Tamia and this certain ball player were hooking up behind my back and cutting me out of the deal. I was pissed but laughed knowing I was going to get the last laugh. I never called them out on their betrayal. One day, I just so happened to run into his wife at their family boutique. I might have asked if they were separated because I had seen him downtown with some young chick. She went the fuck off and while her family and friends tried to calm her down, I snuck my ass right out of the shop. Two weeks later, Tamia was found dead. I never saw that shit coming, but how long did Tamia think she could get away with being sneaky? That's it, that's the story.

That afternoon, I went home with two, new, pretty faces for my party.

Trina

It had been two long weeks since we did that party at Candy's house, and I'd only been on two dates since then. The money I made at the party helped out so much, but after paying for my classes, I was dead broke again. So, doing this next party was a must because I still needed my books for these classes. Since meeting Candy, I had slowed down with these dates after seeing how much I could really make in one night. Truthfully, for some reason, I just wasn't in the mood to continue with this lifestyle any longer. My plans were to do just a few more parties and get the fuck on. I was using this Candy shit as a steppingstone.

I noticed things had been changing around here, and I wasn't sure if it was my attitude of doing something I didn't wanna do anymore or Eve's new attitude, but she really had been getting on my nerves. Lately, her new best friend was Candy, and I didn't like it at all. She really said fuck school and was out here tricking just to shop. I wasn't sure if Candy was playing in her head or what, but she was doing too much just not enough. I wasn't jealous that Candy was using her as her go-to girl for extra jobs, but the way I looked at it, Eve jumped headfirst in the game and it wasn't a smart idea. Yeah, we were both selling pussy, but she had Candy hooking her up on private dates and shit with all these weird ass men. She was doing too much, and I hated to see her like that. Just the other night, she came home and could barely walk. She had to soak in the tub for hours just to get the swelling to go down. Crazy part is that Candy called her the next day. Not to make sure she was alright, but to trick her out again.

Out of curiosity, one day I asked Eve how much money Candy made off her dates, and she couldn't even tell me a straight number. I always tried to be straight up with my girl, but when it came to Candy, she was blinded by her bullshit.

"Where are you headed to?" Eve asked, standing in my doorway.

"I wanted to go get my nails done so I won't have to rush at the last minute. Party in a few days," I said dryly.

"Damn, bitch, what's the fucking problem?"

"Nothing at all."

"It doesn't seem that way. Say what you gotta say and say it with your chest."

I had to laugh at her ass. "Ok, Ms. Big Bad Ass. You wanna know what's the problem? Come over here to see."

I led her over to the mirror.

"Bitch, look at you, you're the problem. I think you're really losing focus on what's important in life."

Eve turned to face me. "Getting money is what's important to me. Bitch, you trippin'. What happened to my bitch that wasn't scared to get these niggas' bread?"

"I'm still that girl, but you've been on some wild shit lately."

"Whatever, girl. You ain't nobody fuckin' mama. Matter of fact, I do believe that all good things must come to an end, and the way shit looks right now, we're outgrowing each other. Things are only gon' get worse if we continue to be friends."

"What are you talking about, Eve? We've been girls since forever, fuck wrong with you?" I questioned.

"You're jealous of me because Candy fuck with me the long way. Then she hooks me up with muthafuckas that are cashing me out."

I couldn't help but to laugh at her although I was dead ass serious. "Jealous? Really, Eve? Did you forget we both were doing the same shit? You wanted those extra dates while I decided not to do all that. I was the one that only wanted to do the parties. And as far as you fuckin' with Candy the long way, I already know y'all fucked. I just thought you didn't wanna talk about it because you were embarrassed or something, so I never brought it up."

"Whatever, bitch," Eve said, walking out of my room.

I didn't even wanna be in the same house as that stupid bitch. I couldn't believe she thought I was jealous because she fucked Candy. I was pretty sure Candy fucked a lot of hoes that she pulled in to work for her. The way I was feeling, I didn't even wanna be bothered with Candy or Eve, but I knew I would be a fool not to do this party this coming weekend. This one weekend could either make me or break me.

Being pissed off, I didn't even leave the house. I spent the rest of the day lying in bed, watching old love movies.

***

The next day, I got up to handle my business. After getting my nails, lashes and eyebrows done, I felt pretty again. I was ready to go home and relax, but I still needed to find a sexy outfit for this weekend. I swear it felt weird doing all this shit without Eve by my side. We'd always been each other's support system, and now I wasn't even sure if we were friends after our last argument.

Since she recently bought a car, I knew she was probably out and about and could pull up. I took a seat on one of the benches in the middle of the mall to give Eve a call. Having beef with someone that I called a sister for years was lame as hell to me. We had a bond that should be able to overcome anything. At least that's what I hoped. After the third ring, she finally picked up. "What's up?"

"What are you doing?" I asked.

I knew she had an attitude when I heard her breathing hard as if I was bothering her.

"I'm actually waiting on my date to show up. What's up?"

"I was about to look for an outfit for this weekend and was just trying to see if you were available to shop with me."

Eve laughed. "Girl, you kissin' ass better than the nigga from last night. You was on that bullshit talking to me like you were better than me when you out here sucking and fucking for money just like me. I don't do fake shit, bitch."

Eve hung up after that. Before she did, I could hear Candy's stupid ass laughing in the background and that's really what pissed me off. I wasn't worried about her talking shit. It was the fact she had a fucking audience that I didn't like.

"Trina!" I heard someone call out.

I turned around to see a guy named Jarrod walking my way. I really wasn't in the mood to be bothered with anyone at the time, but since I had a crush on his sexy, black ass, I waited.

"Hey," I softly said.

This man did something to me that I couldn't even describe. No matter how many men I slept with throughout my life, Jarrod was the one who could've got it for the freebie.

"Hey, girl," he said, pulling me in for a tight hug.

The smell of his cologne instantly turned me on. I always had a thing for a nigga that knew how to dress and keep up with their personal hygiene.

"What you up in here grabbing?"

I couldn't tell him I was on the search for a hoe outfit, so I lied. "I was looking for an outfit for a friend's birthday party."

"I bet whatever you find, you'll look good in it."

This dude knew what to say to make a girl blush. Everything was perfect, but he was barking up the wrong tree. Yeah, I wanted him, but Jarrod deserved someone without a large body count. He didn't seem like the type who wanted to wife a hoe. He deserved much better, no matter how much I liked him.

"I gotta go," I said, getting in my feelings.

"Aye, wait a minute," Jarrod said, grabbing after me.

I stopped to see what he had to say. It's clear that we liked each other, but I couldn't be the bitch to bring him down.

"I was thinking that maybe we could grab something to eat since we're both here."

Maybe next time. I thought it was cute how he was trying to get on. I pretended to give it some thought before telling him a bold face lie.

"I'm sorry, Jarrod, but I have somewhere to be."

The look of disappointment was all over his face, but I needed to push away.

"Why don't you give me your number so I can call you? Then maybe we can see what day we both are free and can go out."

I didn't wanna get him caught up in my lifestyle, but at the same time, I didn't wanna just shoot him down knowing we were feeling each other. I needed to get my shit together and soon. After letting my hand go, we exchanged numbers. I walked away feeling like shit. I kept telling myself that after a few more parties, I would be straight, then I'll be able to live my life for real.

I left the mall without an outfit after all that shit. Between Eve's bullshit and feeling embarrassed talking to Jarrod, I just wasn't in the mood anymore. To be honest, I was ready to slap some fucking sense into Eve's childish ass. And if Candy had something to say, I'd slap her ass too.

After getting home, I was still pissed. I found myself pacing the floor, questioning my whole life. I fucked around and made a living out of selling pussy, but I was old enough to know it was wrong. Then I had the nerve to be embarrassed about something I could have easily changed. I was a fucking mess. I sat there for a whole ten minutes looking at Jarrod's number, trying to build up the courage to give him a call. Truthfully, I would have loved to have a life outside of selling pussy. Here was a guy who actually liked me, and I was trying to push him away. I couldn't help but to shake my head at my damn self. I gave his number one last look before pressing talk on the phone.

"Hello," I heard him say after the third ring.

"Hey. Are you busy?" I asked, using my sexy voice.

I could hear him moving around as if he was leaving out one room and entering a new room for privacy.

"Not at all, what's up?"

"My plans fell through at the last minute. Did you wanna meet up somewhere?"

He paused for a minute, but I could tell he was smiling. "Yeah, that sounds like a plan."

We decided to meet downtown at Hart Plaza. In the hood, Detroit wasn't really shit, but there was always something to do downtown. Once downtown, we met up just in time for things to start popping off for the African festival. We walked around holding hands and talking about life. I had to keep the conversation on my future because talking about my past or my life right now would scare him off.

Feeling my phone vibrate, I stopped mid conversation. "Hello," I dryly said, seeing it was Candy calling.

"Hey, Trina, have you heard from Eve? I have a client here waiting for her ass. She was supposed to be here twenty minutes ago and isn't answering her phone."

Rolling my eyes, I quickly said no before hanging up. Candy then texted my phone.

Candy: There's no beef between us, sweetie.

I quickly texted back.

Trina: Of course not, see you this weekend.

I put my phone back in my pocket, feeling Jerrod eyes staring at me.

"You don't have to go, do you?"

With a warm smile, I told him no.

At the end of the night, he was nice enough to follow me home, but we didn't do shit but kiss each other goodnight. That night felt magical without all the sex and everything. I knew that I needed more nights like that in my life.

Eve

The last time I talked to my best friend Trina, I was such a bitch to her. Now here I was, laying on this floor, bleeding out, praying I make it out alive.

Earlier that day, I had been talking my shit to Trina, then I decided to be a bigger bitch and go to the apartment. I knew that she wasn't there, so I wasn't worried about shit popping off between us. After tearing up the apartment, I packed my shit to move out. I had already talked to Candy about crashing at her house for a minute until I could find a nice place to live.

Not thinking clearly, I tore her room up looking for her stash, but only found $75 in her dresser. That bitch was broke, broke. She wasn't even on my fucking level.

I had just placed my last bag in my trunk when I heard a familiar voice call out my name.

I shut my trunk then turned around, rolling my eyes.

"What do you want, Marcus?"

"You've been on my mind. I just had to come see you since you blocked my calls and texts from your phone.

I shook my head at this man. He just wouldn't give up for shit. "I told you I was done with you. Now go home to your wife."

"I'm trying to make you my fuckin' wife. Why can't you see how much I love you?"

"Marcus, I don't have time for this shit," I said, turning to get back in my car.

I intended to drive away from him so I could make it to my date that night, but Marcus had other plans for me.

I felt a cloth cover my mouth and nose, then everything went black. I didn't even have time to fight his ass back.

***

When I came to, I didn't even remember what the hell happened or where I was at. That was until Marcus walked into the room. This crazy muthafucka had me tied to a chair in his fucking dining room. Across from me was a heavy set, older, white lady. I assumed it was his wife, Tammy.

"Marcus, what are you doing?" I asked.

"We need to get some shit together tonight. I refuse to continue to be unhappy."

Tammy tried to wiggle out of the rope that held her down, but of course, she wasn't going nowhere. Shit, neither was I.

"Marcus, what is this all about?" she asked as if she wasn't scared.

Marcus paced the floor. "Tammy, I tried to do this the easy way. I told you I didn't love you, and I wanted a divorce, but you wanted to make shit harder than it had to be."

"You're my husband, Marcus. We took vows to stay together until death do us apart."

I sat there wondering why I was the only one really freaking out. This shit was nowhere near normal.

"Marcus, this has nothing to do with me. Please take me home."

"That's where you're wrong, Eve. This shit has everything to do with you."

"Untie me, Marcus," I demanded.

"I can't do that, love. I know you'll run away without letting me explain everything."

I was scared and instantly started crying. "Marcus, I wanna go back home."

"Shut the fuck up, Eve. You know how much I love you, I'm not gonna hurt you."

Us being tied up didn't seem to piss Tammy off that much, but him saying that shit drove her over the edge. She started acting like a mad bull trying to get out of the chair. This bitch was ready to kill me.

"You love this black bitch? Is this why you want to divorce me, Marcus?"

"Yes, Tammy. Damn! Just sign the fuckin' papers so me and Eve can live our fuckin' lives in peace!" he yelled.

"Marcus, we can't be together. I told you that before."

Marcus walked over to me and placed a kiss on my lips. Something I'd never allowed him to do. "You said we couldn't be together because I was married. I'm showing you that I'm trying to get rid of this bitch right now for you. I love only you, Eve."

"Untie me, Marcus, I'm getting scared."

Just as he started to free one of my hands, Tammy began yelling again. "Marcus, you have lost your fuckin' mind. Untie us and take that little bitch home!" she demanded.

Marcus was able to untie one hand before he walked over to Tammy.

"Eve, will you marry me? I'll get rid of her just like I promised."

"Can I go home?" I cried.

Marcus surprised the fuck out of me, and I felt so bad for Tammy.

"Tammy, if I untie your ass, you gon' sign these divorce papers?"

Tammy was a bold one and didn't fear this crazy muthafucka. "I'm not signing shit so you can be with your little whore."

Marcus didn't hesitate to pick up the butcher knife that was on the table. He looked me straight in my eyes before splitting her throat. Her blood was everywhere, and I lost it. After a loud scream, my tears ran out a little harder.

"What the fuck Marcus?"

He walked towards me holding the knife. "We can get married now, Eve. She's out the picture."

"No, Marcus." I continue to cry.

"I can take care of you now. It's just us now, love. I'm gonna take good care of you," he said, giving me another kiss.

Hearing noise coming from the back room, Marcus ran to the back to see what was going on. Because one of my hands was already free, I quickly freed the other. This man was crazy, and I couldn't end up like his wife Tammy. Just as I hit the living room, I heard Marcus call out my name. Instead of stopping, I took off, trying to make it out the front door.

I never made it out the front door. Matter of fact, the last thing I remember before everything went black was hearing the gun shot before it hit me.

CHAPTER NINE
Trina

I guess Eve was really pissed at me because she had moved out. I tried calling and texting her ass over the last few days, but she wasn't reaching back out to me. I wasn't about to beg the bitch to come back home or anything, but I was gonna let her know I was gonna fuck her up for fuckin' this apartment up. I honestly felt like if she wanted to move out, she should've just done so instead of touching my shit. Bitches be petty as fuck when you call them out on their shit.

My phone started going off. Me thinking it was Eve, I quickly answered, ready to go the fuck off.

"Hello."

"Turn on the news!" Candy cried into the phone.

In my gut, I started to feel sick and didn't want to see what Candy was talking about, but I turned the news on anyways.

As I listened to the reporter discuss the story of the murder/suicide involving three adults and one child, my heart dropped, and I couldn't stop crying.

"I'm so sorry, Trina, I really am," Candy said in between her cries.

I didn't want to hear shit from her, so I quickly hung up the phone.

After the story went off, I had the understanding that the white dude that was in love with Eve had kidnapped her. His sick ass killed his wife in the dining room then went in the room to kill their child. Eve was found dead at the front door, so they thought she was trying to escape when he shot her down. Marcus loved Eve so much that he laid next to her before blowing his brains out.

Eve was all I really had in this world, and now she was gone. I couldn't do shit but cry my eyes out. What was I supposed to do now without my sister by my side? We might not have been on good terms when she was murdered, but that was and would always be my fucking sister, blood or not.

I eventually cried myself to sleep and when I got up, it was already dark out.

I felt like someone was watching me 'cause as soon as I got up, my phone started going off.

"Hello."

"Trina, where are you?" Candy asked.

"I'm at home, just got up."

I heard her smack her lips. "The party has started and you're late. With Eve no longer with us, I have something lined up for you."

I shook my head. "Bitch, are you fuckin' crazy? My fuckin' sister was murdered, and you actually think I give a fuck about your damn party? Fuck you, bitch."

"I was only trying to help your broke ass out, but fuck you, broke, stupid, loose pussy thot."

I wanted to go off again, but she hung up.

I sat on the couch and cried my eyes out again. Life wasn't fair at all, and this was a hard pill to swallow. Hearing my phone go off again, I decided to ignore it. I figured it was Candy calling back to talk more shit. She must've really wanted to get shit off her chest because she called right back.

"Hello."

I then heard Jarrod's voice. "Hey, Trina, I just heard about your friend. I wanted to call and check on you."

I couldn't even respond. All I could do is cry into the phone as he listened. He stayed on the phone with me the whole time I had a breakdown, which I appreciated so much.

"I'm outside your apartment if you need a listening ear or just a shoulder to cry on."

I took him up on his offer and went downstairs to talk to him. I liked him, and in a way, I was using him as an escape from reality. In a way, I think he knew but didn't mind as long as he could be up under me. We sat in the parking lot just talking, but mostly, he held me as I cried over Eve.

Just as I decided it was getting late, and I needed to go in, I noticed Eve's car parked a row over. Her keys and purse were still sitting on the seat.

"This shit so bold, Jarrod. She didn't deserve this shit!" I cried.

He held me in his arms, repeatedly telling me to be strong and that everything was gonna be alright.

"Before I leave, I'll help you bring her stuff into the house if you like."

I shook my head in agreement. Jarrod did as he said he would do before leaving me. I spent the rest of the night going through her things and playing a memory game in my head. Everything that she packed up reminded me of the good times we shared. My tears turned into giggles as I thought back to all the crazy shit we'd been through together.

The last bag I needed to go thru was smaller than the rest. Unzipping the bag, I found the rest of the money she had left over. Knowing she didn't have a family, I was gonna use the money to have her cremated. Something in me wanted my sister with me at all times.

Two Weeks Later

I was able to put together a small service for Eve. The little family she did have didn't show up, but some of the students from our school came to show some support, which I really appreciated.

One day, Jarrod called me out of the blue just to check on me and to get me out the house. I had been in the house depressed and in my feelings. I wanted to shoot him down, but I could hear Eve telling me to get my ass up and go see what that man wanted.

I got dressed and met him downtown. As we walked around Hart Plaza, he held my hand and just listened to me vent about everything that I was feeling.

"You still plan on attending school this fall?"

"I thought about taking the semester off, but I know Eve would haunt me every night. I was the one damn near forcing her to be in school. She wouldn't want me to just quit," I said, giggling.

Jarrod smiled. "I'm happy to see a smile on your face. You're truly beautiful, Trina."

"Thank you, Jarrod. I appreciate you being there for me during this shit."

"You know I like you a lot, and I know some shit about you, but that's not pushing me away. I don't want you to ever think I'm judging you on anything."

I stood there in disbelief. I wasn't sure how he knew, but the fact that he still wanted me is what puzzled me.

"Jarrod."

"You don't have to say anything about that shit if you don't feel comfortable about it. I only brought it up since I felt like you were pushing me away because you were embarrassed about that part of your life."

I was really embarrassed now and couldn't help but to put my head down. Jarrod lifted my head, placing a kiss on my lips.

"It's time you be with a real man who's gonna help you overcome whatever had you doing what you were doing. You too fuckin' smart to be out in these streets like that."

As he held me, I cried tears of joy.

***

Over time, things were going good between me and Jarrod. That fall, we walked to class hand-in-hand. I was happy with him, and he was the best thing that'd happened to me in a long time. He'd been there for me whenever I had a breakdown thinking about Eve. What I loved about him the most is that although he knew about my past, he never brought it up or even wanted to talk about it. He loved me for me, and that's exactly what I needed in my life.

One night, while doing homework, my phone went off. Thinking that maybe it was Jarrod calling to tell me he was downstairs, I quickly answered.

"Hello."

"Party starts at 8pm, I expect to see you there."

"Candy, I'm not doing no fuckin' party. I'm no longer in that type of lifestyle. Bitch, stop calling me!" I yelled into the phone.

"I have men that paid for new faces, and you didn't show up. And we both know why Eve wasn't at the last party. Bitch, you owe me."

I gave it a good thought. "What time did you say it was starting?"

"I said 8. Bitch be on time and be ready to work." That said, she hung up the phone.

I had no plans on showing up to that bitch's house. I waited for Jarrod to show up so I could go over my plan with him.

"Babe, that sounds like a good plan. You ready to get this show on the road?"

With a smile on my face, I quickly said, "Yeah."

After making my important phone call, we chilled, waiting for everything to unfold.

It took some time, like a whole four days, but I was happy with my work. Me and Jarrod laid across the bed watching the Channel 2 Breaking News.

Reporter Shelia Smith reported about the bust of a prostitution ring that was raided just days again. She then talked about all the low lifes that were cheating and spending all their money for a good night. Candy's picture flashed across the screen as the Madame that ran everything. She had a few charges against her ass, especially when they took out some underage girls at her last party.

I couldn't help but to laugh. Hopefully, these women could find a better way of living.

"Good job, baby," Jarrod said as I laid on his chest.

"Thank you, baby. I couldn't have done this without you. I love you, Jarrod."

"I love you too, baby."

Let's Chat

1). Is there really such a thing as easy money in your eyes?

2). Trina was ready to walk away from that type of lifestyle. Do you think she should have followed her first instinct?

3). Do you feel like Candy tricked them to work for her?

4). Candy had a messed-up past. Do you think that's why she acted the way that she did?

5). Do you think Eve was leading Marcus on?

6). Did you think Marcus was gonna snap the way that he did?

7). Do you think Trina would ever go back to selling her body?

8). What are your thoughts on Jarrod?

9). Was Trina wrong for snitching on Candy's parties?

10.) Do you think that because Candy had messed around with Eve, that caused Eve to believe that Trina wasn't a friend anymore?

11). What were your thoughts on Maria?

12). What were your thoughts on Jasper?

Email me your answers at Messiah.nf@gmail.com

T. Friday was born and raised in Detroit, Michigan. At the age of 36, she is the mother of five children. Three handsome boys ages 19, 15, and 13 and two beautiful girls ages 10 and 8.

At a very early age T. Friday became in love with reading books such as Babysitters Club, Sweet Valley High and Goosebumps books by R.L Stine. It wasn't until she was in her early teens when she was introduced to Urban Fiction books. That's when she knew that she wanted a career in the book industry. January of 2016 T. Friday had her left leg amputated and that was when she realized that she had been taking her life for granted and it was time to make her dreams come true. She picked up a pen and some paper then started writing. In May of 2017 T. Friday signed her first contract with Racquel Williams who is the owner of RWP. Now in 2021 she is the author of 26 books. She has plans to continue writing until one day all of her books are turned into movies.

T. Friday's Book Catalog

Intrigued by a Savage's Love (Standalone)
Finding Love in a Real Boss 1
Finding Love in a Real Boss 2
Nasir & Kennedy: Luv in the Gutta (Standalone)
In Love with a Street Princess (Standalone)
To Be Loved by a Brick Boy 1
To Be Loved by a Brick Boy 2
To Be Loved by a Brick Boy 3
Yearnin' for the Love of a Thug (Standalone)
All Cried Out: Lovin' a Detroit Nigga 1
All Cried Out: Lovin' a Detroit Nigga 2
When Love Calls the Shots (Standalone)
Saving all my Love for a Young Boss 1
Saving all my Love for a Young Boss 2
Jewel and Javarri: His Love Wasn't Enough
(Standalone)
Tears Shed from Loving a Trap Nigga 1
Tears Shed from Loving a Trap Nigga 2
A Detroit Nigga Finessed my Love (Standalone)
Pretty Bitches get Even (Standalone)
Aaliyah & Marcel: Side Chicks Wanna Be Loved
Too (Standalone)
Prettier in Pink (Standalone)

Boo'd Up With a Young Outlaw for Christmas
When a Street King Wants You
Upgraded to a Real Boss
Upgraded to a Real Boss 2
Thot Girl Summer Detroit

Author's Contact Information

 Author T Friday

 Authortfriday

 @TFriday9

 If you haven't already signed up for my email blast for new updates on all my books Messiah.nf@gmail.com

ALL MY BOOKS CAN BE FOUND ON AMAZON.COM
Read a book, leave a review on Amazon or Goodreads, and tell a friend.

* 9 7 9 8 8 2 0 2 9 1 6 3 0 *